Against all odds:

A subconscious account from Valerie Ann Thompson

By

Lowe Ashley

This book in its entirety is a work of fiction. Any names, characters, places, and events are products of the author's imagination or are used completely fictitiously. Any similarity to authentic events, locales or persons—living or dead—is wholly unintentional. This is a promise to you, the reader, from me, the author.

Young Adult Reading Material

LGBTQ Reading Material

CHAPTER 1

What is a Simple Life?

I grew up thinking that life would be so wondrous. I could be whatever I wanted to be. Well, that's according to my parents. And, of course, that plan had to fit into whatever they wanted to me to be. I hate feeling like I have to make my parents happy.

Planning would make everything fall into place smoothly. I had everything scheduled from a very early age. I had my best friend, Ali, always at my side. We have always been inseparable. We were going to go to college together. Ali and I were sure we'd end up getting jobs doing about the same thing. We'd always been fascinated by movies and wanted to work behind the scenes.

We'd both live near each other-- hopefully somewhere with a beach-- so that we could live the BFF life.

 If there's one integral piece of information that I've learned in my twenty-five years on this planet-- things don't always turn out the way you want them to. In fact, most of the time, you never even come close. Why couldn't I have figured that out a lot sooner?

I'm trying to calm myself down in the back of this horrible, dimly lit limo. I can't stop fidgeting with the silver tulle under my white gown. The gown was so white it reminded me of the blinding effect snow was capable of having on my eyes. How poetic? I'm wearing an angelic dress for my special journey to Hell.

I couldn't stop thinking that I'd rather be at home. My favorite jeans and a comfy t-shirt were waiting for me. I could almost hear them calling my name. I could almost feel the comfy flannel wrapped around my body.

Instead, I was going to be attending my own funeral in this silk and lace disaster. "This is the worst day of my life," I think to myself. This day was never a fitted piece in the puzzle of my grand master plan. With the way the laws were heading, a marriage would never be in my future.

Let me clarify one of my previous thoughts. I realize this may be slightly confusing. By funeral I actually mean that it's my very own perfect, princess wedding. You know, the one that every girl spends her nights dreaming about. The one that girls make believe about during their entire childhood. No expense has been spared for this day. My parents have gone all out, emptying three savings accounts for the dress alone. I don't even want to consider what his family has put into the affair. A typical, traditional wedding had no place in my life or in my dreams.

I know what you're thinking. It sounds weird, right? Most women are more than happy to be getting married. They're ecstatic beyond all reasonable, and sane, belief. Those women even go to great lengths to become Bride-zillas. They make their bridesmaids insane with their every whim. And, of course it had to be the way they wanted it. Well, I am an exception in this particular design. I don't even know where I'm getting married. Hell, I have no clue what anything even looks like beyond this limo and the dress I'm wearing.

Women generally look forward to the honeymoon and the life they want to lead after that. Girls stage pretend weddings from a young age. Teenagers doodle Mrs. Last-Name-Goes-Here all over notebooks in middle and high school classes.

There's only one problem. I have never been like any of them. In fact, those were the girls that despised me growing up. Why? I'm different.

My groom-to-be, Tom, is a wonderful person. He really is. He's very handsome and extremely smart, which are all pretty nice characteristics for a man to be granted. He's always been sweet, but kind of pushy with what he wants. He's not too patient at all. He's got a good head on his shoulders and he's very successful.

Let me just break it down for the entire world to hear. Tom is just not what I want. I'm not even interested in him in the slightest way. Let's just say that Tom is not my type. But, if I were to tell him or my parents that, I'd be found dead. That's if I was ever even found at all. Isn't that a fun thought to be thinking about when I'm supposed to be looking forward to the happiest day of my life? It's just wonderful being me.

CHAPTER 2

Tom and I Cross Paths… Unfortunately.

Tom and I met during my summer interning as an assistant to the director of a film he was starring in. I was getting the director a cup of coffee when he bumped into me, spilling the latte I had worked so hard on perfecting. Without apologizing, he said, "I'm Tom."

He was very matter of fact, as if he really needed to introduce himself to me. I didn't let him know that I already knew exactly who he was. He was the guy that all the girls would talk about. Who could miss the marvelous celebrity? He's been in every mainstream film since I could remember.

Tom sort of stalked me for a few weeks after that. Okay, not sort of. He full on haunted me wherever I was. It was kind of cute at first, but I still wasn't interested. I had a certain someone else on my schedule. Plus, I'm not exactly what he, or anyone else thought I was.

My life has always been a big act of show and don't ever tell. People like me are not as widely accepted as we should be. Everyone has their secrets, right? My secrets could have me detached from my family completely. My parents are not very forgiving or tolerant of people that choose not to hold the same values that they do. Case in point: me.

I came home from a long, hard work day—of mainly fetching lattes and rounding up actors and actresses for the director-- to find him sitting on the overstuffed couch with my parents and Ali. That was the couch where I had my first intimate

moment with the one I truly loved. That was the couch that we had watched our favorite movies on. That was my couch. That was my home. And, Tom had invaded my space for the last time. I was planning on telling him off the moment I saw his face. But, my father interrupted my big moment.

Dad popped up faster than I have ever seen him move and said, "There you are, sweetheart. I'm so happy for you. It's about time you settled your life down and found a real man."

I stopped dead in my shoes. I'm fuming. "Umm… What do you mean 'found a man'?" Up to this point in my life, I've never even had a boyfriend. Some kid—I can't remember his name—in first grade kissed me on the cheek once. That didn't turn out well for him. And, I'd hardly consider that a boyfriend since I beat the snot out of his face. He never talked to me again, by the way.

That was also my first trip to the principal's office.

My parents were so pissed that I wasn't even allowed to go to my forced ballet classes. I still feel like I won that battle in a round-a-bout way.

"Tom here told us the news! When's the big day?" Keep in mind, this is the happiest I have ever seen my father. He didn't cheer me on at my softball games. He didn't approve of me being in liberal clubs in high school. He wasn't even excited that I brought home a four point four grade point average in my AP courses. Mom had to force him to go to my ballet recitals. He's not the interested-in-your-life type of dad. Well, until now.

"What big day?" I asked in an awkwardly high-pitched squeal, eyebrows arching as high as my forehead would allow. Could anyone tell I was seething on the inside? Was it me or was there actual steam billowing from my ears? My heart pounded. That had to be visible in the vein in my forehead that made its grand appearance every time I got mad. Right?

Tom and I had had very little interaction outside of the coffee incident. In fact, I tried to avoid him all together. His creeper tendencies had started to annoy me after the first week. Sending flowers and balloons to my home was uncalled for. Following me around set was even offensive. How'd he ever figure out where I lived anyway? What news could he possibly have to share with my family and Ali?

Why was Ali here for Tom's big announcement? The thought just crossed my mind in that moment. Tom hated Ali. In fact, Ali hated Tom just as much, if not more. They had never even spent more than ten minutes in the same room before. I'm pretty sure it's because her and I are so close. From my observations, we're the only two women at the set that completely ignore the fact that Tom even existed. The tension in the air was as thick as a heavy rain in the dog days of summer. Add some mosquitoes and it was just as annoying.

"Tom said you two will be getting married, dear," Mom said rather bluntly, pouring drinks for everyone in the room. Trusty old Mom. She is a heavy drinker. All she does around the house is drink and watch the soap operas. Every now and then she'll have her book club over for tea and discussions. As a matter of fact, I haven't seen those ladies in months. I don't think she ever cooked, either. She's always been on the liquid-lunch diet. She tended to leave everything for the nanny to do up until the day she left. I had been wondering why Dad lost so much weight. Makes sense now.

Mom never wanted me to work in the first place. According to her archaic philosophies, women graduated high school, got married to a man and had that man's children. There was never even a college option. Then, those same women stayed home forever to take care of those kids, with the help of a nanny. End of story. No questions asked.

Mom has never believed in an educated, working woman. Needless to say, she's not thrilled with the life I had chosen lead. I'd hate to demolish what little positive opinion she had of me by telling her the truth. Hell, she was livid the day I announced I'd been accepted into the university. I couldn't imagine the hell I'd pay if she ever found out the truth. You should have been there for the "I quit ballet" talk.

To be honest, I've always loathed my mother and her special ways. I wished that I could just rebel against her. Unfortunately, if my actions were to hurt my mother they would also hurt my father. I would never want to do that to him on purpose.

I've always wanted my dad to be proud of me. I just never seemed to be good enough for him. So, I would always just stick with whatever made them happy. And, what made Mom happy, made Dad happy. That way he wouldn't have to deal with her shit.

I couldn't tell them the truth about myself and I knew it. I couldn't tell them what I really wanted from my life. I tried going down that road before, but it never worked in my favor. I couldn't tell them about the person that I really loved. I'm lucky I survived my mother after I told her that I would be attending courses in a college.

There was no escaping Tom's forcible entry into my life at this point. As everyone stood to hug me with congratulatory praises—except for my mom—I tragically collapsed into their embraces with my eyes closed and fists clenched tight. I had to figure out a way out of this.

CHAPTER 3

Why Would Anyone Purposefully Walk Straight Into Their Nightmare?
The door of the limo opens and the sunlight hits my eyes. I squint and look out to see if anyone is around.Thankfully, the whole walkway is absolutely desolate. Not a single person is around to see my misery. My face feels tight with too much makeup. I can feel my entire face caked. There's no way my skin is getting any air. I can't breathe wearing this stupid corset. I look ridiculously fluffy from the waist down.

Is this how women really like to look for their wedding? It feels terrible.

Inside the church I have my own room waiting for me. Casually making my way to the door, a horde of women I don't recognize rush forward on me. I can't make out a single word they say because they're all talking at the same time. Something about my hair isn't right. One of the ladies pokes and prods at my head to fix it. My dress apparently isn't fluffy enough. Another woman proceeds to further fluff me up. Another lady talks about the color of my eyes and how it doesn't work well with the makeup.

This blob of estrogen forces me into the tiny vanity chair in the antique room. Here comes more makeup. I want to scream. I just can't win. I knew I should have stayed in the damned limo.

It should not even come close to amazing me so far into my life but the cattiness and hatefulness of grown-ass women makes me laugh on the inside.

'Give me a fucking break, ladies!" I think to myself. Oh, how I wish I had the audacity to say it out loud. They fuss and bicker at each other about what works and what doesn't. Who cares? I don't even want to be here anyway. Let me look like crap. Maybe Tom will let me go.

Finally, there's a face I recognize from the corner of my eyes. Ali is the most naturally beautiful woman I have ever had the pleasure of laying my eyes on even from peripheral view. She smiles and holds her arms out as she runs towards me in her shimmering, light blue gown.
"So, I guess the colors they're going with are light blue and white?" I ask her. She's been more part of this event than I have.

"I don't know. I just know that I'm wearing this fabulous dress," she says and then sticks out her rosy tongue. I have to admit, it is pretty silly looking on her. We're not exactly dressy girls.

I have to admit, though. Ali's bridesmaid dress is perfect. I just never thought I'd see the day where Ali would even look at a dress. She's hates them. Thousands of tiny crystal-like sequins glisten in the sunlight coming through the barred window just behind the vanity. Her blonde tresses—held in place by similar looking crystal pins—are curled and tiered, outlining her face and neck. I can honestly say that Ali is the only girl I have ever been envious of. Her stunning features make mine look dull and drab. I'm so ordinary compared to her. My face is easily forgettable. Her gemstone eyes make my dingy, mud-colored eyes look like trash in comparison.

"You don't look happy," Ali says to me. Her eyes barely glisten in the lighting coming from above the vanity mirror. Those eyes can make any room dazzle, though.

"You know that I'm not happy with this, Ali," I say as I look down at my hands folding over themselves anxiously in my lap. She knows that I'm not happy. She knows why I'm not happy, too. This shouldn't be a surprise for anyone involved, other than Tom and his family. "This isn't how I planned things would be."

"Val, I know. It's frustrating to see you this way. It makes me so sad. I feel like there's nothing I can do to help. I just want everything to be okay." Ali closes her eyes and puts her head in her hands. Ali has always been easy to read. She shows her exasperation by clutching her face in her palms.

Even though she's wearing a dress, she doesn't bother to cross her legs or her ankles like the rest of the women in the room. It is the little things that I love about her, really. Her knees are spread wide open as her elbows rest on them. She knows there's no need to be ladylike around me. I let a small grin streak across my bright red mouth. "I don't mean to make you sad. You know that I don't love him, though. My parents…" Ali nods her head in response to my statement without letting me finish my thought. It's the unfortunate truth. She goes back to fussing over my hair and makeup and we play this game where we try to make each other laugh. We both know it's not working, but we fake it for each other anyway. I fake it for her.

"Your lips are way to red for your skin tone," she says, mimicking the voice of one of the older ladies that were in the room.

The rest of the bitter, old women come back in and flush me into the hallway that leads me down the aisle to the minister. Is he a minister? I don't know what to call him. Is it even a man? It'd have to be right? I'm so new to this stuff it makes me sick.

I stumble a little, tripping over my over-flowing gown. I regain my balance and stare ahead at the massive and ornate mahogany door that is the portal to my future. I hear the organ begin to play a melody that sounds all too frightening and familiar. I feel like I'm going to have a panic attack. I haven't eaten in days and I still feel like I could vomit. Oh, how joyful.

I look around to see if there are any doors or open windows I can run to. At the end of the hallway to my left is a window. There's no promise of it being unlocked, though. To my right, there's a different door. Again, there's no promise of it being open, but it's worth a shot. Something has to give. There's no way in Hell I could make it back out the front door where I originally came from.

Ali is just a few steps in front of me waiting for the door to open so she can begin the procession. Her foot taps in the silver high heels the ladies picked out for all to wear. The spike of the heel looks like it may be made of diamonds or crystal. My shoes are similar, but why did I get stuck with the highest heels of them all? I think I got hosed on this decision. I'd rather be barefoot.

That's another thing I never expected her to wear. Ali is known for only wearing her pink and black Converse shoes-- the ones with no laces. Every now and then she wears some black flats or flip flops. Seeing her in heels is just so weird.

The rest of the ancient women are all lined up behind me. My mom is holding the train of my wedding gown. She admires the intricate lace and patterns of crystal beads. I can see her smoothing the fabric beneath her fingers, loving every square nch of the wedding dress she picked out. She probably secretly wants it for herself. That's completely okay with me, too. She can have it. I hate the dress with the passion of a thousand fiery suns at this very moment.

And, just then, in that moment, I get a great idea. Mom, can you spread the lace out on the floor? I want to see it again before I walk down the aisle," I ask her as casually as I can manage. I don't want to make a scene just yet. She lowers herself to the floor, softly patting and spreading out the train. I leisurely turn to my right as if I'm going to look down at it. "No sudden movements, Val," I say to myself under my breath.

"What's that dear?" my mother asks, looking at me with slanted eyes.

"Oh, nothing. I was just thinking about how pretty the pattern is." Yeah, right. Don't get me wrong, the pattern is beautiful. It looks like vines and leaves and petals and flowers woven into a web of fabric. But, it's really not my style. I definitely don't do silk or lace, let alone the color white.

Under the dress I carefully lower myself out of the too-high heels, instantly making myself about three inches shorter. Grabbing as much of the dress as I can in two fists, I rush and make a break towards the closed door down the hallway. Running as fast as this stupid, fluffy dress will allow, I slam face-first into the door. Thankfully I couldn't run too fast.

I'm not sure if, or for how long, I was unconscious. The next thing I know I'm shouting various obscenities when I look up to see the ladies gathering around me. There's a little bit of sparkle around them in my peripheral vision. I can see the stars that everyone always talks about. My forehead throbbed with pain. The damned door was locked. There will be no escaping this day. Just lovely. It's just my luck, too.

"I have to use the restroom," I tell them firmly in order to sway them from believing I was trying to run off. I'm not sure how I'm keeping up this confident, cool act. Everyone that knows me knows that I am not the gutsy one of the group. My childhood goldfish had more guts than I ever have. Don't even get me started on how clumsy I am.

My mother shot me a glare that meant I was dead if I tried anything funny like that again. She's on to me. She knows. That woman scares the shit out of me. I think she may kick puppies and eat kittens in her spare time.

I'm telling you, she has some of the most sinister looking deep brown eyes. I don't think I've ever actually been able to distinguish her pupils from her irises. Mom's eyes are so dark they look like they're completely black. Her eyes almost look like they are the same shade of tiny onyx marbles. She's always terrified me with those looks. I'm honestly not sure what my dad has ever seen in her.

When I returned to my place in line from my faux-bathroom break, the organ was still playing and the doors just began to crack open. After scrutinizing my face and slapping powder on my cheeks and forehead, everyone rushes to their places behind me all over again. It's time to begin my descent into my own personal hell.

CHAPTER 4

The Worst Day and the Best Day All in One -- Is That Even Possible?

The colossal, ornament of a door opens slowly into the main area of St. Mary's. I have never seen the inside of a church before.This room seems too big to be real. The cathedral opens up to a high vaulted ceiling. Painted glass windows surround the entirety of the church from front to back. The windows look as though they have angels in various poses on them. They're absolutely beautiful. The pews are the same mahogany the door is made from and not any less decorative. They send an off limits vibe. The walls are an off-white that seems to have been stained with time. Everything looks antique. Everything seems incredibly untouchable. I should not be here. I'm just waiting for the hall to burst into flames.

Ali looks back at me with a fake smile and I see a tear run down her left cheek. Before turning back around to complete her stroll, she looks helplessly at the crimson velvet carpeting and stops smiling completely. "She's given up," I say to myself in the abyss that is my current state of mind. I hate when she looks like that. Deep down inside, all I want is to be next to her to tell her that everything will be okay and that we can still move forward with our original plans and ideas. But, I can't because I feel like it's never going to be okay.

Walking down the aisle to the minister-- I'm honestly not sure what to call this man, and he is, in fact, a man-- and my future husband is like walking to the gallows and the executioner. My life is over. There's no question about it now.

I let myself fall into a daydream about when Ali and I were younger and in high school. There was this one day that I remember most fondly. It was after school and we sat in the meadow out beyond the football field. The grass gave us enough cover to hide from the rest of the world. Nobody would ever be able to see us there. This was one of the only spots where we could be ourselves.

We'd bring notebooks, pens and cameras that printed photos on the spot. Ali and I would write stories about our future selves. We would get caught up writing poetry to and about each other. I still treasured the scrapbooks we made each other for our birthdays. When we went to college together, that all stopped, but we still had other means of sticking together for our best friend time. College meant that we didn't need to sneak around to be together.

The only other place I could think of as wonderful would have been the beach off Lake Michigan. Hanging around the dunes all night was just as fantastic as the meadow by the school. The only people that went out there late at night were the ones that wanted to get away. They were our people, even though we never spoke to them. They were just like us.

The smell of the sea air is my most valued recollection of that time. Any time I've ever had the opportunity to smell it, I close my eyes and I'm immediately brought back to those days. Now, it just makes me sick with aching and longing for those times to come back to us.

I'm not a kid anymore. There will be no sneaking out with Ali to sit on the beach dunes, talking until the sun peeps up at us over the horizon. There will be no sneaking Ali into my room at night when my parents are asleep or away. There will be no more Ali and I alone together at any point in time. My life, as I know it, is truthfully over.

I snap out of my reminiscing and back into my real life issues. This is horrible. What is it that I used to love writing in my notebooks? "Reality is a lovely place, but I would never want to live there," I think to myself. How fitting that phrase is for today?

Tom stands there smiling his big, tacky smile. His shit-eating grin makes me shudder in disgust. His teeth are the whitest teeth I've ever seen. They are absolutely unreal. He has the fakest smile I've ever witnessed on any human being. I guess it helps that he's pretty well known. People clamor over him to get his teeth that clean and picture-perfect for movies and photographs. The funny thing is that his face is nowhere near as perfect. It's a phenomenon what special effects and makeup can do. It is such a waste of time and money.

My very own personal procession comes to a stop long before I do. Each woman stands in their designated spaces to the left side of the smaller, more arched shelter on the stage. I have to keep moving forward to my position about ten feet in front of us. I trip slightly on the tulle beneath the dress. I catch myself from falling and continue on. I'm so freaking clumsy.

The lights go dim and the music halts sharply. The silence is overbearing. I can actually hear people breathing in the pews. The only bright lights in the entire church are the ones focused on us, and the single spotlight concentrated on the crucifix just behind the man about to sentence me to a life of marital misery.

This may be blasphemous to think, but Jesus looks like he's crying and mourning for my soul just as much as his own. For a moment, I feel bad for him. Then I remember where I am and what's about to take place in my own life. Now, I feel bad for myself and I begin to pray that this all ends as quickly as it started. What's funny is that I never pray for anything. If there is a God, maybe he'll grant me this one wish.

I sit and wait for my prayer to be answered. But, nothing ever happens. No sign is shown. I'm screwed.

We both look at the priest and he solemnly begins his speech in an eerily robotic voice. You know the one. It's all too excruciating to listen to or repeat.

I tune him and everything around me out as if nothing else in the world exists. I pretend that none of this is even happening and put Ali's face where Tom's is in my mind's eye. This magnificent image gets me through until Tom interrupts my thought process with a gruff cough. I guess it's my turn to repeat those dreadful words. We echo after him and he orders the man to kiss the bride, totally and utterly sealing my final fate as Tomas Espinoza's wife.

Tom lifts the white, lacy veil from in front of my face. His smile has faded into a forced, narrow gaze. He deliberately leans in with his eyes confidently closed. His smug façade inches closer, ready to slap his smooth, glossy lips on mine for the first time. Yes, he's about to kiss me for the first time ever. How on God's green Earth could we be getting married if we've never even smooched? That's not the first absurd red flag in this series of events.

I shoot a quick glance at Ali. My movement catches her eyes. As if she's reading my mind, she throws her bouquet towards the crowd of onlookers and races towards me, snagging my hand in hers.

It's all as if it is in slow motion. Time seems to freeze while I watch her come at me. We yank each other back down the aisle towards the russet door, losing both pairs of our shoes on the way out. I hated those things, anyway. I am much more comfortable with my feet touching the ground beneath me.

People try to corral us away from the exit. They attempt to block our paths. People try to snatch us by our gowns, but we let our dresses tear nearly clean off our bodies in order to ensure that we liberate ourselves from this mess. We flash by each pew of people as we run for our lives. I can feel my mother's stare drawn down on the back of my neck. I've never felt so petrified in all of my life. It takes all of the energy I can muster to endure and carry on.

We push through the giant front doors of St. Mary's Catholic Church. Thankfully the limo is right where it was when I left it. I trip and fall to my knees just after stepping from the last step of the stairs that lead away from the church door. Ali yanks me up and we dive head first into the parked limo. Ali cries to the driver, "Paul, go! We have to go!" The doors lock as the driver, Paul, looks back at us in confusion. This is the first time my life has ever fallen into such chaos.

Once the car starts progressing down the street we sit back and attempt to relax, watching the people filing out of the ever-shrinking church behind us. Former friends and family run after us as we break away from the curb. The ladies desert their position in the mad pack first. The men chase us for another block and slowly start dropping out of the race. Eventually, they all stop running after us. Looking back again, I see that there are a lot of phones to ears and thumbs twitching and sending texts. I immediately switch my phone to the off position.

Ali and I look at each other. She grips my gloved hand and we bust out with the hardest laughter our bodies could possibly create. We fall over each other's laps as tears of joy and celebration stream down our makeup-packed faces. This is the worst day and the best day of my entire life, all solidly rolled into one. Maybe my life's not over after all. Is that even possible?

CHAPTER 5

Shall We Head Out?

The next morning, I can't help but think to myself, "Was this all a dream?" I can't believe I managed to abscond from my own wedding. Am I still alive or was I murdered and guided up to some glorious version of Valerie's Personal Heaven? Either way, I'm not complaining. I'd usually slip on my Vibram FiverFingers, but they're somewhere back at my parents' house. Instead, I peel off the stockings from yesterday's nightmare and head out the door with my key to get a quick run in before Ali wakes up.

The morning's dew was still fresh on the ground beneath my feet. I love the feeling of the soft, wet grass between my toes as I run through the morning mist. Barefoot running has been my private therapist for the past five years or so. I feel like the great Mother Earth understands me better than I understand myself most of the time. It's scary, honestly.

The air is nice, but a little thick this morning. It's a tad foggy out, which adds to the excitement of running through the morning haze. I never really know what's around the next corner as I course through the rounds of today's jog. The light wind has a slightly flowery scent. I can't seem to place what the smell is exactly, but it reminds me of the fragrance of flipping through the pages of an old, worn book.

Coming back into the hotel room, I try to be as quiet as possible. I see that Ali is still sleeping the early morning away and her body is splayed across the bed. She is still stagnant, lying in the same position as when I left this morning. I sit down on the edge of the bed closest to her head and run my fingers through her tangled hair.

My own stirring about the room must have woken up Ali. She sits up on her lean elbows under the covers and looks at me with this perky, cheerful smile. Only she can light up a room with the slightest twitch of her lips. That's always amused me. I get a warm, fuzzy feeling in the pit of my soul every time she beams.

Ali's long, champagne-like hair is a tangled mess. Her makeup is still caked but smudged all around her striking face. Even though she doesn't believe me when I tell her, I still think she's more beautiful when she wakes up than anyone else I have ever met. Not that I've ever waken up next to anyone else, but the thought must count for something.

What's the best part about all of this? Yesterday wasn't a dream at all. I'm resting next to the most bewitching woman in the universe. I'm the luckiest lady on the face of the planet.

"Good morning," Ali says to me as she settles into a sitting position and yawns, stretching her arms high above her head. "Well, I think we need to get organized and plan out where we go from here. I don't really care to stick around too much longer."

"First thing's first. I need to get rid of this phone." I throw my iPhone on the bed. I turned it on this morning to a massive influx of missed calls and text messages from people that were once my friends or family. Most of the calls were defamatory and cursed me to Hell where I must have surely come from. Oh, well. Mom, Dad and Tom were not on that list of missed calls, thankfully. "Hey, since when are you the planner? Isn't that normally my job?"

"Ha ha, very funny. Oh, and great idea. Definitely lose the phone. And, let's hunt down some breakfast first. I'm starving."

"Not for me, thanks. I'm not all that hungry," I say as I gently lay my hands on my distressed stomach. It's the truth. I haven't been truly hungry in weeks. Everything has been weighing down on my mind and the stress eventually killed my appetite. Now there's this whole new pressure to deal with. What have I done? I feel sick with nerves.

"Listen, Val, don't worry about them. We'll head south and they'll never be able to find us. We'll do whatever it takes. We're both better off this way and you know it," Ali says seemingly frustrated with me. I'm always the wimp. I'm the first person to get frazzled over any minor setback in plans. I know this was all sudden and it's difficult for her to get a handle on, too. Deep down, though, I know she's entirely dead on. She's always right and sometimes that kills me.

We get up out of the warm and comforting bed. The hotel cleaning ladies left our invoice under the door. I bend down and lift it up off the burgundy floor and throw it in the trash. We gather our things and get dressed in the clothes that Paul, the limo driver, had brought us the night before when he dropped us off. I had stored a pre-packed gym bag with my wallet, a few pairs of jeans, a couple t-shirts and plenty of underwear in the front of the limousine. You know, just in case.

I have a habit of planning for any possible situation I can imagine, even some that are not quite in the stars. Don't get me wrong. I wasn't planning on running away during the wedding. I had actually been planning my evasion once we ended up in Peru for the honeymoon. If I couldn't escape, I certainly would have died in the forest trying. Anything would have been better attempting to live a life where I no longer existed. Now, I just wish I was smart enough to take the plane tickets from Tom prior to leaving. Ali and I would have had it made!

Fortunately, I have been able to save up quite a bit of cash rather discreetly. I don't think anyone but the bank knows about my checking account. I'll tell Ali about it all eventually. The internship was a salaried summer job before my final year at the university. I had been living with my parents and they pretty much paid for everything I needed at the house. I was able to pass the job off as a traditional, unpaid internship, so everything went to the bank save for a couple dollars here and there. If my math is correct, and it always is, I have enough to get us to Florida, Nevada or Calgary before we really need to consider earning an income.

CHAPTER 6

Coming Up With the Diner Plan

At the diner down a few blocks from the hotel, Ali and I grab coffee, omelets and bacon for breakfast. I'm only eating to make sure she eats at this point.I know she's hungry otherwise she wouldn't have brought it up this morning when we woke up in the hotel room. I feel bad that she has to play any part in this mess. At the same time, I am feeling guilty because I couldn't do it without her.

For the most part, we are very quiet. Neither of us says too much to each other. We're too consumed by our thoughts to speak. For the longest time, we just sit there. I play a spoon through the eggs on my plate and sip at my coffee. It's getting cold. Ali puts down her fork, takes my hand softly in hers from across the table and gazes right through my eyes.

"I have an idea."

"Okay! That's what I like to hear. Come on, out with it," I put down my fork and wipe my mouth with a napkin, ready to listen to anything that could come out of her mouth. Any idea has to be better than no idea. I'm too fuzzy to properly think about any solution to the situation we have found ourselves in. I am happy to know that she's capable of thinking when I am so obviously not.

"I don't know about you, but I have money saved in a bank account. I don't know how far it will get us, but I think we should get as far away as we can and fast. I'm kind of weary of people like Tom. You know the celebrity-types."

"Oh, we'll be fine. Before too long, they'll forget all about us."

However, I can't help but agree with Ali for the most part. The longer we stay this close to Tom and my family, the more definite my demise is. I know my parents will either come after me or completely disown me. One way or the other, there's no point in staying around if I'm not wanted here. I nod my head and ask, "How do you think we should proceed?"

She pauses to think about the question for a few seconds. "We've always said we would like to take a road trip after college. It doesn't look like either of us will be going back to finish out our senior year any time soon."

"Great point," I say, putting the cold coffee mug up to my face. "But, I can't go back for my car. We won't have any way to get ourselves on the road."

Ali grins mischievously at me, shaking her head and rolling her eyes like she already has a plan put together in her beautiful mind. I'm obviously of little use in this conversation. She's always been good at being bad. I don't thinks she's ever been caught for any wrong deed she's ever committed.

"My car is pulling up now," she says as her brother and his girlfriend pull up in two separate cars in the parking lot right outside of the grimy diner. One is Ali's old, black Ford Focus ZX3. I'm seriously surprised she still has the car. It's only a few hundred years old. Okay, I'm exaggerating. She has had it since she was sixteen, though.

"Do you think we'll really be able to get far? I don't want to take any chances getting caught," I say. I'm always the responsible, motherly figure. I'm also the biggest worry wart I've ever met. Sometimes, I wish I could be more daring and adventurous like Ali. If I had to choose, she'd be my idol. Earlier in our conversation, I wasn't too cautious about avoiding Tom or my parents. Now that Ali is talking up getting away, I feel a little more nervous.

"We'll be fine. Nobody knows what I drive. We always take your car, Ms. BMW." She has a point. Since I bought my BMW-- partly due to Tom's insisting and my dad's credit-- we never had a need to drive her crappy Focus. Err... I mean, that lovely little Ford she loves to drive.

"Perfect. Let's go," I say, gesturing to the door. I stop and pay for our meal at the register before I make my own exit. We didn't really have a waitress, so I didn't bother leaving a tip. Plus, I don't think we'll ever need to worry about anyone spitting in our food here. Chances are we will never be coming back. At least, that's the plan.

Outside in the parking lot, Ali's brother, Mark, and his girlfriend, Amber, were getting out of the vehicles. Ali gave Mark and Amber a long hug,

thanking them for their assistance. I have never met Amber before, but she seems
nice enough. I grab Mark and hug him, too. "Thank you. You have no idea how much I appreciate this! I owe you big," I say as I pull away from his embrace.

"Don't worry about it. Anything for my sisters," he says. We all laugh and Ali motions for me to get in the car. We can't waste too much more of our precious time. I do love how Mark has always been the best big brother I've never had. He was our hero growing up. I can't believe I'm admitting this, but we used to wear his clothes and pretend to be his little brothers.

"Thanks, again, Mark!" She screams out the window as we pull out into the street in front of the diner. "I'll call you guys when we get where we're going!"

She sits back and lets out a deep breath. "Where are we going?" I want to ask. I look over at her wavy, blonde hair flowing out around her tanned face. She pushes a golden lock back behind her left ear exposing the small, heart-shaped tattoo on the side of her neck.

Looking over at me with a flirtatious grin she murmurs, "Ready?" Her eyes put me in a brief trance. I can't help but sit there and look at her. She snaps her fingers in front of my face.

"More than you know," I say as I grab her soft hand between the grey cloth seats. "Did you let Mark know where we were heading? I ask.

"No way. I don't even know where we're going for sure. I have my cell if he wants to talk. I told him I'd let him know where we ended up so that they could come visit."

Along the sides of the highway, there are seas of wildflowers growing. There are specks of white here, purple there and yellow littered everywhere in between. The breeze smells a bit like the trees around the neighborhood where we grew up.

"I'm ready," I whisper to myself.

CHAPTER 7

Emergency Services to the Rescue

I slept in the passenger seat for a few hours and then woke up to Ali singing in the driver's seat as we pulled into a gas station. She has the most beautiful singing voice. I could also be biased, though. "Where are we at?" I ask her, rubbing the sleepiness from my eyes. I look at my reflection in the window and see that my makeup is running down my eyes.

"We're somewhere south of Cincinnati. I'm pretty sure we're getting close to Lexington. We've only been gone for a few hours though," she said like she knew where we were headed to. We had decided, before I fell asleep, that we'd just head south and see where that takes us. She adds,

"According to the map on my phone, I-75 takes us all the way to the Gulf of Mexico."

"Florida it is then. It's my turn to drive. Take a break," I say as we both open the car doors to get out and stretch. "Do you want coffee or anything from inside?" I ask as I shrug towards the gas station. "I'm going to get myself some caffeine. I have a feeling it's going to be a long night."

"French vanilla, please. Could you grab me a bag of chips, too?" She asks, batting her eyelashes at me. She always knows just what to do to make me melt. Ali is a Funyuns fanatic even though I don't think the taste goes well with vanilla coffee.

"Of course," I say. I flash a smirk and a quick heart shape with my fingers across my chest. "I love you," I think to myself. I wish I had the courage to tell her how I really feel. I'm not sure it's much of a secret, though. I don't think it's ever been a secret. She has to know, right?

Back in the car, I set our coffees in the cup holders. A little French vanilla spills out onto the black plastic of the middle console where the emergency break is. Ali grabs her cup and takes a swig. She swallows it quickly and then opens her mouth to say that it's hot, but she doesn't make a sound. She waves her hands around her mouth frantically trying to cool her burning tongue.

And then, her arms drop to her sides and her eyes fly wide open. The coffee spills all over the seat and the floorboards at our feet. The hot coffee scalds my toes and I jump back from her side of the car.

"Fuck!" I yell. I don't mean to yell at her, but the stinging won't go away. After calming myself for a split-second I take a quick breath. "Are you okay?" I ask her. "The coffee is hot. That's kind of why they put the label on the side of the cup."

"Put the car in gear! Put the freaking car in reverse, now!" She screams at me, her eyes gaping straight forward through the windshield.

A black Escalade flies into the gas station straight towards the nose of our car. I put the car into reverse and drive backwards as fast as I can almost hitting the gas pump behind us. I do take out a trashcan, though. I curse under my breath and secretly wish Ali was driving the car.

After a quick donut behind the gas station, I put the Focus in drive and haul ass down the street. The SUV sails after us as I push the limits of the puny car. We wouldn't have this problem in my BMW. Why doesn't this thing have turbo-mode or something?

Ali keeps a look out through the back window, eyes locked on the SUV targeting us. "They're gaining speed. I don't think this piece of shit can outrun that thing," she says with tears streaming down her eyes. "What're we going to do?"

 I don't even have a second to think. I have nearly zero time to react. I can't waste any more time. I fly back on I-75 and push towards Lexington. According to the signs, we're only about thirty minutes away. If we can just keep ourselves engulfed in enough traffic, our small car should be able to lose the massive SUV. "I think I have a plan," I tell Ali, trying to calm her down. I'm not too confident about it, though.

"You think you have a plan? There's no time to think!" Ali screams. Her stream of tears has turned into a river and she's sobbing. "We've got to get out of here. Who knows who the hell they are! Get us out of here!"

"Don't worry, Ali. Everything's going to be okay," I lie with a grim smile. I hate lying to her, but I don't have a choice. I'm not sure that everything is ever going to be okay at all. Obviously not buying what I'm trying to sell her with words, she keeps yelling at me.

Just as I finish my sentence, the Escalade collides into the trunk of the car sending Ali and I crashing forward. From the corner of my eye, I see her head whip towards the dashboard. My face slams onto the steering wheel. I can only see the crimson canal washing through my eyes. I hear the crack of my nose before I feel it. The blood gushes heavily from my nose. Ali dangles loose at the restraint of her seat belt. She's nothing but a ragdoll.

I scream for Ali to wake up and try to watch the road at the same time. I wipe my face with the sleeve of my sweatshirt furiously but nothing gives. All I can see is red. The driver of the black SUV steers the monstrous vehicle into the driver's side of our petite car. Everything is moving in slow motion. Our small, dingy-black heap of metal—crushed in on the side and rear end—careens through the guard rail and flips into the ditch between the interstate and the woods around us.

My body is jolted out of the seat and up against the seatbelt that's doing its best to hold me safely in the car. Glass smashes and shatters all around me. I see Ali's body loose and her arms flying around the passenger side. Once the car comes to a stop upside down, I grab Ali's hand to make sure I can still feel her heart beating. There's a pulse but it's weak.

"Hang on, Ali. You have to stay with me," I say knowing she won't be able to hear me. I unbuckle myself from the seat and fall to the roof of the car.

I kick out what is left of the window on my side of the hunk of smoking scrap.

Ali's face has blood flowing down from her once flaxen hairline. Her eyes are squeezed shut, but she's slowly coming to. "Ali, we have to get out of here," I whisper quietly, trying to be as silent as possible so that nobody could hear that we are still alive. "Ali, come on. We need to get into the woods!"

Just then, from the direction we crashed from, I hear a car door slam and two men talking amongst themselves. "There's no way anyone could have survived that crash," One says to the other. I can't see who they are from inside the car. They stop at the top of the ditch and continue talking about the wreckage they must see below.
"Ali, they're coming! We have to move to the trees. Now!" I'm no longer whispering at this point.

"I hear voices down there. Come on," the other man says to the guy that was previously talking. I hear their heavy footsteps coming down the side of the ditch. They're approach is faster that I would prefer. There's no chance for us to make our escape into the woods. Ali is still coming back from unconsciousness when the two men show up here at the debris.

"Is anyone in there? We need to get you out of the smoke. Say something."

"I really don't think you heard anything, Randy. There's no way that anyone could have survived this. They tumbled at least three times. Everything's shattered. I can't even tell what kind of car this was," the man says back to the other guys. He looks down into the over-turned car and I catch his eyes through the busted glass.

"Please don't kill us," I say, clenching my eyes closed. I'm hoping that they'll either make it quick for both of us or, at the very least, let Ali go. I have a funny feeling that I'm not going to get off as easy as Ali might.

"Why would we kill you? We saw you crash and just want to help."

Once Randy and Russell, brothers from Lexington, pulled me out of the car, I rushed over to try and get Ali out. There's no way that I'm leaving Ali in there any longer than I have to. We got Ali out, somewhat safely, and laid her on the grass near the edge of the woods. She points a trembling hand back up the hill to the interstate and starts to moan out some imperceptible words. The man in the black Escalade was standing next to his vehicle on the side of the road. When he noticed that he was spotted, he climbed back into the SUV and sped off down the Interstate. "I have a funny feeling that's not going to be the last of him," I say to nobody in particular.

"Do you guys know him?" Randy asks.

"I have no idea who that guy is. He chased us from a few exits back and rammed us from behind. Then he hit us from the side and we flipped into the ditch," I said to Randy while Russell was calling for emergency services.

The ambulance and police arrive on the scene shortly after Russell hung up his phone. "They're going to want to know everything," Russell says to me, looking at Ali's near lifeless body.

What am I going to tell these people? I'm never going to be able to tell them the truth. My entire life is spiraling down around me and I still have to keep up this game of charades. Does anything ever get easier?

"Ali, you have to stay awake. Stay with me, Ali." I slap her on the cheeks and shake her a little bit by the shoulders. The paramedics run down the hill towards us with a gurney for Ali. "Everything is going to be okay, Ali. You have to wake up." The paramedic and EMT take her body from my arms. The police bring me a blanket and Randy and Russell help me up to the rescue vehicle. "Thank you, guys," I say unsteadily. My voice cracks and trembles as the words flow from my mouth. I don't even feel like I'm the one talking. I almost feel like I'm watching myself speak to these men from above.

They nod and return to their lives and the road knowing they saved two young women from a car accident. What they don't seem to realize is that they may have just saved us from being murdered.

Who was that guy and what did he want with us, anyway?

CHAPTER 8

He Knows, Ali. He knows.

In the back of the ambulance, Ali is still out of sorts. The paramedic said that I could ride with her until we get to the hospital. He said there'd be no guarantee that we'd get to stay together while Ali gets fixed up. He cleans up my own face, and then starts to wrestle with Ali, making sure she's as comfortable as she can be. I don't think anything could make her comfortable right now.

The paramedic finished hooking Ali's arm up to the IV and moved to the front of the ambulance to let us have our privacy in the back. He didn't recommend it, but he caved after I explained what happened and that we were together. It was actually the first time I've ever been able to mention to another living human being that Ali and I are together as a couple. Even though, technically we're not. A girl could dream, right?

I reach for Ali's hand but she's slightly faster than I am. I'm terrified I'm going to hurt her just by touching her. She clutches my cold fingers first. "Is he still following us?" she asks me softly, writhing at the pain the slight movement caused.

"I don't think so. I saw him pull away from the side when he saw us looking up at him." At least that was the truth. I hate that I've been lying to Ali so much. I feel just as terrible knowing that I'm going to have to keep the acts up, too.

"So, he knows we're still alive," she says while she tries to scrape away the dried blood from my hand. She doesn't have to explain to me why she said this. I know she's worried that he'll be back. I'm worried about the same thing. This isn't one of those things we can just magically put out of our minds even if we do try to.

"Unfortunately, yes." Ali looks at me with knowing eyes. I don't think either of us really expected for any of this to happen. It wasn't supposed to go this far. We were supposed to get safely away and move on with our lives. We wanted to be invisible to everyone. We wanted to be forgotten. I don't think Tom is going to let any of that happen. If this was his doing, he's made that answer quite apparent.

"Did you see who he was?" Ali asks, looking down at the tubing that protrudes from her vein. Blood trickles down the side of her arm near where the needle went in.

"I saw him, but I don't know who he is." I don't think to mention that he's probably been sent by Tom. I don't want to do any more damage than what has already been done. The less she worries and thinks the better off she'll be. "I'm sorry that this happened, Ali. It's completely my fault. If we would have just stayed…"

"Don't be sorry. We couldn't have stayed and you know it. We're in this together," she cuts me off abruptly. She lets out a cry from the pain in her chest and bends in a half attempted version of the fetal position.

I know she doesn't want to hear what I'm going to say next, but I have to say it anyway. I need to get it off my chest.

"But I never meant for you to get hurt."

"Listen," Ali says sternly as she fails to sit up in the gurney, "I'm fine. We're fine. We're both still alive. All that matters is that I'm here and you're here and we're together. We're alive." She breaks down into a sobbing mess of tears and torn clothing.

"Ali, you're not fine. You're hurt and it's my fault," I say.

I lean over and hug her as gently as I can. The paramedic says it's likely that she sustained a few broken ribs. She'll definitely need stitches to close the wound from when her head hit the dashboard. My nose has already been fixed by the EMT that was with the paramedic. If that hurt as much as it did, I can't image the agony that poor Ali must be going through right now.

This is the worst part, I think. I barely have a scuff on my forehead and a busted nose. I never wanted Ali to get hurt. I'd do anything to take her pain away. All I have to deal with is a broken nose and a couple of scratches on my forehead. She may have a concussion and all kinds of other issues.

What if she died there in that car? I should never have gotten her into this mess with me. If I would have just stayed there at the church, Ali would have been safe and completely unharmed.

I'm torn over all of this. If I would have stayed, Ali and I wouldn't be able to be together. I know Tom wouldn't even consider letting me be her friend. Don't get me wrong, he has no clue about how much I love her, but he's obviously the jealous, vindictive type. But, if we would have stayed, she'd be safe and free to live the life she wants. Neither of us would be running. I feel nauseated and confused.

"Ali," I start to say, but she puts her hand up to my mouth so that I can't continue to say anything else. I just wish she would let me get it all out. I should invest in a notebook or something.

"Val, stop. Everything is going to be okay," she says to me. I know how this works though. It's the same thing I always say to her when I don't know

how things are going to end up. I try to put a
strong face on for her to see. I know that I'm not a
very good liar. She can see right through me.
She moves my face close to hers so that she can
see my brown eyes look deep into her sky blues.
"Everything is going to be okay," she repeats. Just
as I go to look down at the floor-- my tell-all sign
that I know it's not true-- she lifts my chin and
puts her soft, sweet lips to mine.

CHAPTER 9

Moving Forward With Bumps and Bruises

We're standing around the outside of the hospital when Ali starts looking around frantically. The weather is perfect. The sun shines down on my light skin instantly warming me up to the freedom I've recently created for myself. The lawn is perfectly manicured and the wind smells like the grass may have recently been cut. I love that smell. There's a butterfly floating on the breeze toward the pretty purple flowers near the hospital's entrance. I wonder what kind of flowers those might be.

"Do you see the truck?" Ali asks me, interrupting my thoughts about the weather and surrounding flora.

"What truck?" I ask her as calmly as possible. I know what she's talking about. She's talking about the SUV that tried to kill us the night before. I just don't want to think about it at all. This is me trying to miraculously erase everything from my mind, and hopefully hers.

"The big, black SUV from yesterday!" She punches me hard in the upper arm and then instantly regrets it. She holds her arms to her mangled rib cage. The gauze from the bandages sticks out through the holes in her shirt. Obviously my ploy to sidetrack that conversation didn't work.

"Oh, that one! No. I haven't seen it at all. We need to get out of here before he does show up, though." How many hospitals could there really be in this area? It wouldn't be too difficult for the guy to find us at this particular one if he really wanted to.

I laugh as she retracts from the pain of the punch.
I think, "Silly girl, why would you do that to
yourself?" That leads me to begin another thought
process. "Silly me-- why would I do any of this to
either of us?"
"No shit," she says to me as we start walking
towards a white taxi that has been waiting for us
to pile in. "Can you take us to the bus station?"
she asks the cab driver.

The cabby guy smells like he may have not taken
a shower in a few days. He looks like he's never
taken a shower in his life. His oily, black hair
looks matted with grease. He's missing a few
hairs on the top of his head. Why do men grow
their hair out when the top starts balding? That is a
phenomenon I will never fully comprehend. This
dude's t-shirt is stained with what I hope is
mustard from a hot dog or something. Is he even

wearing any shoes? I do not dare to investigate any further.

"No bus station. Train station, okay?" he says loudly in return. I think there's something in his mouth, too. He spits while he talks. That kind of drives me nuts. I want to yell at him and tell him that we're not deaf and to finish chewing before speaking. What ever happened to manners?

"That's perfect," Ali says looking at me with questioning eyes. I think she's waiting for me to say something about the train. I don't think either of us has ever been on a train before. I honestly didn't even know they still had passenger trains in the United States these days. Is it anything like a subway or a monorail? I guess I'll be finding out.

"You seem to know what you're doing. What's the plan?" I ask casually like nothing out of the ordinary has ever happened. We're just two normal girls out for a fun-filled adventure.

"We don't have a car, so I think the only option we have at this point in making our escape is a bus or train. We don't have the time or money to fly anywhere."

"I think we may have the money to fly, if that's an option. I'm not sure how time really plays into it," I say hesitantly. She's looking at me like I may have lost my mind. "I think we may be too close for comfort. We need to get somewhere very quickly. A plane would be the quickest way to get out."

"You don't think that anyone would be looking for us at the airport?" she asks me, her tone is a little sarcastic. She has the tendency to get cranky when she's tired, hungry or in pain. I want to tell her what I really think. I really think that somebody is going to be looking for us no matter where we go. I don't dare say that out loud, though. Sometimes it's just better to keep my big mouth shut.

"Good point. Train it is." I'd rather not fight with her on this. The cabby whisks us away to the train station, blaring music I cannot seem to make my mind comprehend. The bass is so loud I can feel it in my chest. I'll be honest. I've never understood why people actually enjoy this rap music. Are the lyrics even in English?

"Listen, Val," Ali starts. "I know things are tough and I'm sorry for getting snippy. I'm just really frustrated." At least she can be honest about it. Now I don't feel so bad for thinking those things about her being bitchy.

"I know. Everything is okay. We'll make it through this. Remember, we're together. That's all that matters anymore," I say as confidently and smoothly as possible.

She grabs my hand and lays her head on my shoulder. I know she doesn't believe me. How could she after all of this has taken place? I gently kiss the top of her head. "I love you, Ali," I tell her, quietly whispering the words in her ear. I've been dying for the moment where I could say those three words out loud.

She doesn't respond. The silence is toxic to my already stunned mind and drained emotions. I should have known not to have said anything. I should have just let it go. I'm always the one to ruin something good with something so stupid. Why can't I ever seem to keep my freaking mouth sealed? My heart rises into a lump in my throat and my stomach churns in distress.

I collapse in on myself as she snuggles her nose deep into my neck. I knew this was going to be a crazy spree given our sudden run. I feel like I actually thought I knew what I was getting us into. But, this is so much worse than what I originally expected. Everything seems to be falling apart right in front of our eyes. The worst part is that it's all of my own doing. If there is a God in the sky, he or she should consider helping us out right now. We could really use any support.

CHAPTER 10

The Train Station Platform

The train station is dead. It's a complete ghost town. I must not be the only person on the face of the planet that has forgotten that they exist. I can only see ten people around and six of them seem to be working here. Ali and I join the ranks of passengers-to-be. Nobody stands in the line in front of us."How far can we get with this?" Ali asks, handing the attendant six one hundred dollar bills.

The lady behind the register counts the money that was pushed under the window. "Where do you want to go?" she asks as she paints her fingernails a horrid hue of yellow. According to her name tag, her name is Michelle. Michelle sits and speaks like she hates her life. I can probably understand why. This place doesn't seem to get much action.

"We need to get south of here. Or, west. Anywhere really," Ali says. She looks at the map behind the counter and points towards the Sunshine State. "Is there any chance we can get to Florida with this?"

"Sure. City?" Michelle asks, blowing on her freshly enameled thumb nail. Neon yellow? Yes, I want to say that her nails are this terrible neon yellow. I can't even accurately describe it. I would say it would be like putting neon lighting in a banana, but even that sounds prettier than this horrendous color. I wonder if they match her shoes or something.

I can't help but observe everything around me. It's a curse I tell you. No little detail ever goes unnoticed in my mind. Ali always laughs at for it. Most of the time, she'll ask me what I'm thinking just to make me stop.

"Tampa," Ali rushes. "We'd like to leave on the next train out if at all possible. We're kind of in a hurry."

"Fine. The next train out goes all the way to Orlando. There's a few stops, but you'll get there eventually," Michelle says with an air of apathy, looking at Ali with a glare in her eye and an attitude on her tongue.

"What a bitch," I think to myself. Then I regain my own composure to keep Ali from getting herself in trouble. That's the last thing we need right now.

"Yes, ma'am. We'll take those tickets. Thank you," I say trying to get Ali to back off and calm down. She's clenching her fists. This usually means she's ready to go at it. I'm just hoping there will be no extra drama today. We don't need any fights to deal with. I think we have enough on our plates as it is.

"Here ya go. Change," Michelle pushes the tickets, cash and coins at me forcefully. What the hell? If I don't get Ali to move from the stand soon, I might be the one to snap.

"Thanks," I say with a hollow tone, pulling Ali away from the counter and over to the benches to wait for the train. Michelle closes up shop and slams the window shut behind us.

"What're you doing, Val? Did you not hear the way she was talking to me?"

"Ali, listen," I say sympathetically. Rude people really do tick me off, too. "We've had enough drama for a lifetime in the last twenty-four hours. Don't you think we should lay low and keep everything cool?" Here I go, again. I'm playing the voice of reason despite my real feelings about the situation.

"I just can't stand when people act like that. It pisses me off." Ali slaps her knee in disgust. She continues clenching her fists and throwing her shoulders up into her neck. Oh, yeah. She's turning into Ali Bear.

"I know, Ali. People, in general, always piss you off." I can't help but state the obvious. She's never been good with her social graces. Proper social skills have always been her prime area of opportunity. I'm not sure how she's dealt with me for so long.

"Damn straight," she says with a silly smirk on her face, smoothing her hair behind her ears. I love that silly smile. "Val, about what you said in the cab…" she says, trailing off and not finishing what she has to say.

"What about what I said in the car?" I ask like an idiot. This was probably not the best response I could have thought up in the moment. She looks at me and narrows her eyes sharply. She knows that I know what she's talking about. I've never been any good at fooling Ali. I've never been any good at fooling anyone for that matter.

"Never mind," she says. Her voice sounds deflated. She touches my hand with her pinky. I take her hand in mine and we sit there in silence, looking in different directions, waiting for the train to arrive. After a few minutes, she pulls her hand away from mine and hugs her knees to her chest.

"What's happening to us?" I ask myself in my thoughts. She stands up and runs to the women's room behind us. It's almost as if she can read my mind these days. I'm more confused than ever. I love Ali. She's the one I want to be with for the rest of my life. I have already kind of poured my heart out to her. I could have been more thorough, but what else can I do?

After a few seconds go by, I get to my tired feet and follow her path through the same rusty door. Ali is resting her hands on the bathroom sink, gazing at her reflection in the mirror. She glances at me and stands straight and tall. "I'm a mess, Val."

"You look great," I say, reaching out to touch her shoulder for comfort.

"No, that's not what I mean. In my head I'm a mess. What were we thinking?" she asks me, tears starting to fall down her cheeks. She removes herself from my touch in a sudden jerk.

"Everything is going to be perfect. Things just suck right now. Trust me, I know. But we'll get through it like we've gotten through everything else before this." I can't be too sure right now, though. I feel like she's drifting away from me. I don't think she wants what we used to have. I miss what we used to have.

"I don't know," Ali says, looking down at the ground, kicking her shoes together. I want to tell her that I don't know how things are going to be, either. I want to tell her it's all going to be okay. I want to say so many things to her. This is not the Ali that I know. This is not the same strong and composed woman I fell in love with. This is the little school girl coming out of her. Unfortunately, I can't help but think that her childish vulnerability is kind of cute.

"The train should be here any minute. Are you coming?" I ask as I walk in the direction of the door, knowing she won't stay behind. There's no way she would leave me after all of this, right? I mean, we've already used the money for the tickets. We just need to get on the damned train.

"Okay. Let's go," she says as she buries her hands deep in her pockets. Her blonde locks fall around her face as she pulls her head up to walk forward. "Orlando, here we come." She puts on a face of false sureness. Her body language is giving all of her secrets up.

As I'm pushing the door open, I see a familiar face walk by. Quietly letting the door fall back in place, I force Ali to the side and into a stall.

If you are reading this i supposed you have read completely series one of "Against all odds: A subconscious account from Valerie Ann Thompson" Congratulations & Thanks

I WOULD BE PUBLISHING SERIES AS SOON AS I GET REVIEWS OF PEOPLE TELLING THEY DID LIKE TO READ

IT…THE PRICE? IT WOULD BE ALMOST FREE FOR SERIES 2

www.ingramcontent.com/pod-product-compliance
Lightning Source LLC
Chambersburg PA
CBHW061437160726
47995CB00003B/934